For Anne

Donald Barthelme

THE SLIGHTLY IRREGULAR FIRE ENGINE

FIRE ENGINE

or The Hithering Thithering Djinn

The Overlook Press · Woodstock · New York

SLENDER~WAISTEDNESS
Corseted Divinities with Waspish Affinities
Worrying, Flurrying

One morning in a recent year, a year not too long ago—
the year 1887, to be precise—a young girl named Mathilda
awoke, stretched, yawned, scratched, and got out of bed.

"What shall I do this morning?" she asked herself. "I
think I shall go hooping. This looks like good hooping
weather."

When she went out into the back yard, hoop in hand, she
was amazed to discover that a mysterious Chinese house,
only six feet high, had grown there overnight.

Mathilda was disappointed. She had wanted a fire engine. Even though it wasn't Christmas or her birthday or the day after a day on which she had been particularly good, she had hoped—just a faint, hazy hope—that when she went outside this morning a sparkling red fire engine would be standing there.

"Well, a mysterious Chinese house is better than nothing," she said to herself. "I suppose I'd better go inside and see what strange things happen to me there. Of course this house is rather small. I'm not even sure I can get inside the door."

At these words the mysterious Chinese house began to grow and grow. It grew and grew until it was nine feet tall, and sprouted a Chinese weather vane on top. And there was plenty of room to go through the door.

"Plenty of room to go through the door now," Mathilda reflected. "There's absolutely nothing to prevent me from going inside. Nothing except those strange noises I hear there."

From inside the Chinese house came strange noises indeed—growls, howls, the whispering of elephants, the trumpeting of djinn.

"I'm not scared," Mathilda said. "Very few people are as brave as me." And she walked through the door.

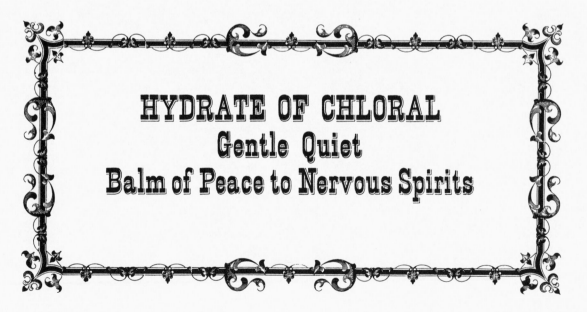

HYDRATE OF CHLORAL
Gentle Quiet
Balm of Peace to Nervous Spirits

Inside the pagoda were two fierce-looking Chinese guards.
"Good morning!" they said in unison. "Who what when
where how?"

"I beg your pardon?" Mathilda said. "Uh . . . do you
have a fire engine in here?"

"No, but we have a rainmaker. Look behind you."

GARDENS WATERED
CARRIAGE-WAYS SPRINKLED
DESERTS DRENCHED

"Pleased to meet you," Mathilda said
to the rainmaker.

"Likewise," the rainmaker said.

"What *else* do you have?" Mathilda asked. "Not that you aren't extremely interesting," she said, turning to the rainmaker.

"Likewise," the rainmaker said.

"Well," the guards considered, "let us see. We have Chinese acrobats. I think that the cat-seller will be around before lunch. We have an elephant that falls downhill, head over heels. That's rather interesting. We have some flying machines, although they're somewhat primitive. We have Chicken Chow Mein. And we have a pirate. Do you want to see *everything*?"

"I think I'd like to begin with the pirate," Mathilda said. "I've never seen a real pirate before."

"He's not in such a very good mood," the guards said. "We captured him some time ago, and he's sort of restless. We tell him that if he just tends to his knitting, he'll be all right. So that's what he does, tends to his knitting. But he's used to a more . . . *active* sort of life."

"The pirate," said Mathilda.

"No interviews!" the pirate cried. "*Especially* no interviews granted to little girls." Then, without dropping a stitch, he began: "The sea was dark. Dark, dark, dark. We were forty-two days out of Port-au-Prince with a cargo of plundered chickens, plundered eggs, plundered silk stockings, and other plunder . . ."

BURIED JEWELS
Oceanic Dredging Company

"A terrible storm arose, and a lady we had on board, a plundered lady, turned absolutely scarlet.

" 'Turn back!' she said to the captain. 'Turn back, or we are lost!'

" 'Turn back?' the captain swore. 'God rot me, madam, if in this wind I can turn any way at all!'

"But we turned back. And the first crack out of the box we were overcome by a Chinese junk, eighty-eight guns, all of the latest make. That is why," the pirate said, "you see me here, knitting."

"I like your beard," Mathilda said.

ANCIENT BARBARIC AMUSEMENTS
For Royalty and the Rabble
Gladiatorial Contests and Encounters with Wild Beasts
Tournaments, Bull Baiting, Boar Hunting

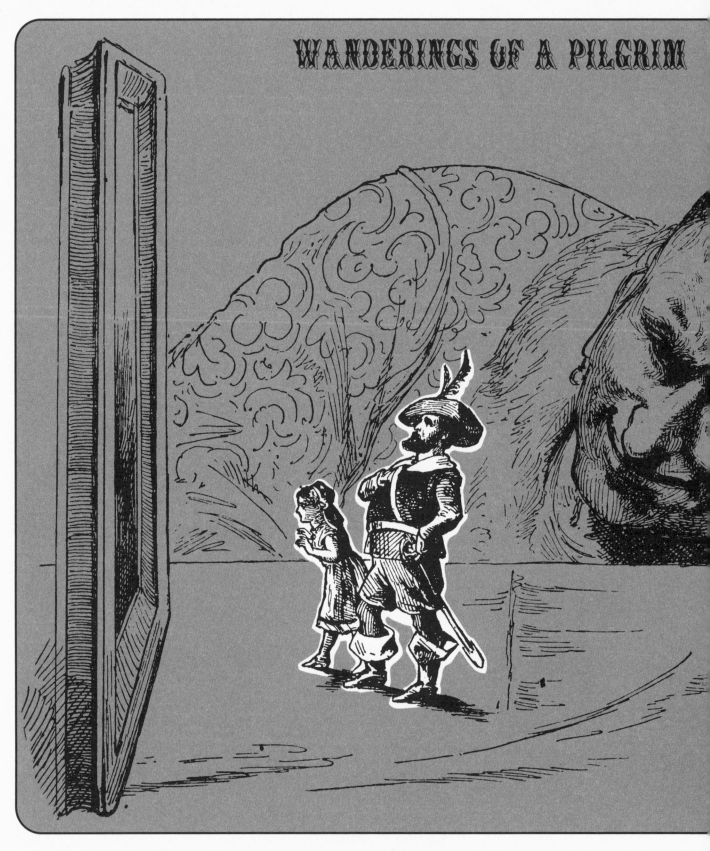

"It's a good beard," the pirate said. "I knitted it myself. I have them in four different colors. Brown, brown, brown, and brown."

Mathilda looked over her shoulder. "Do you get a sort of watched feeling?"

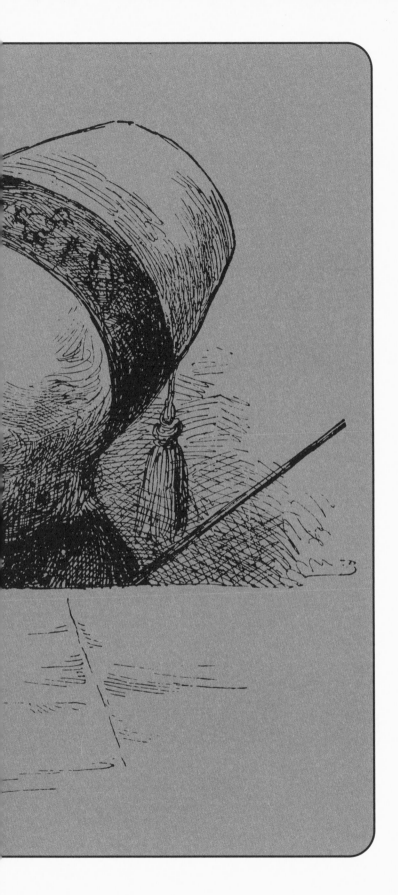

"Just a djinn," the pirate said. "He lives in that jar there."

"Can I meet him?"

"No," the pirate answered. "Come along. A special djinn will show you around. He's the *official* guide."

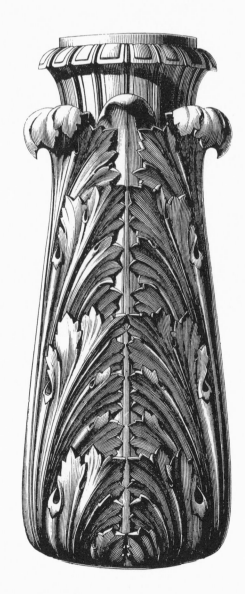

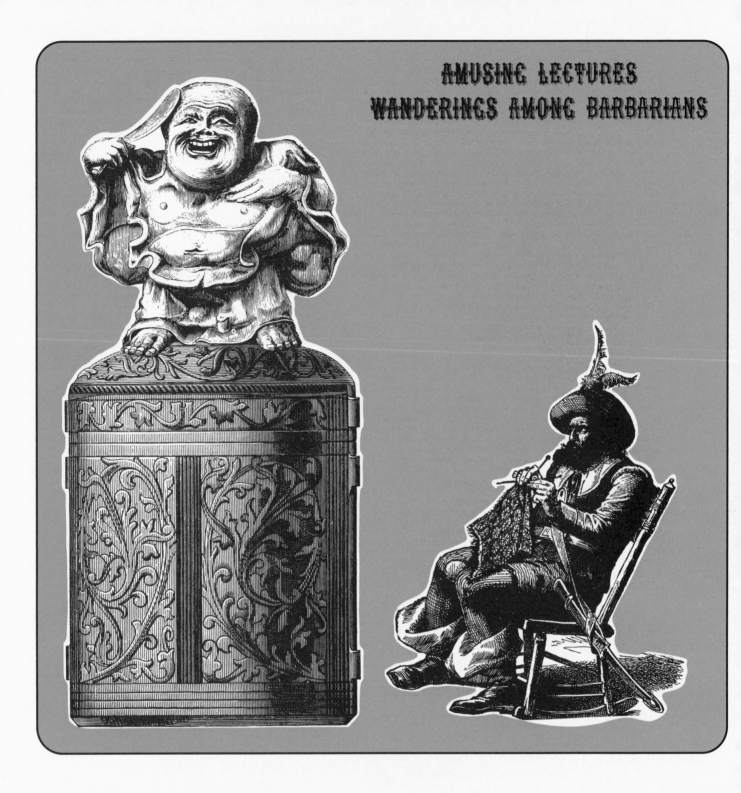

"Well, slap me if it isn't Mathilda," the new djinn said. "Has the pirate been taking good care of you?"

"Oh yes, he has," Mathilda said. "But I haven't seen the fire engine."

"We don't have a fire engine," the djinn said. "Although they're mighty attractive, fire engines. I admit it. But here comes the cat-seller. That means it's just about time for the elephant to fall down the hill. Let's go and watch. He does it very well."

The pirate came too.

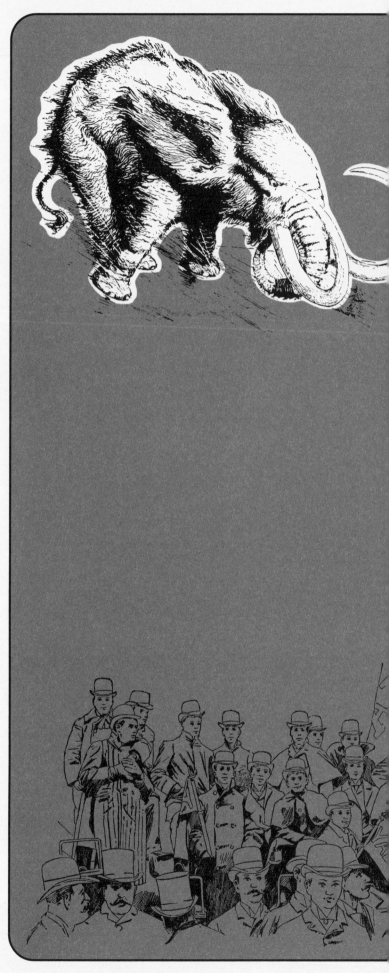

A great crowd had gathered to witness the event.

"He's wonderful!" Mathilda exclaimed.

"An elephant and a half," the djinn said proudly.

"That's not so special," the pirate said sourly. "If you'd give me my cutlass back, I'd really show you something."

"Does he do it every day?" Mathilda asked.

"He is closed Mondays," the djinn replied. "And now, what else can we show you?"

"For such a small mysterious Chinese house, this pagoda certainly has a lot in it," Mathilda remarked.

"We like it," said the djinn.

MODERN ENTERTAINMENTS

Barnumian Charioteering
Trapeze Daredevilism, Pugilistic Ruffianism
Shortgowned Theatricals

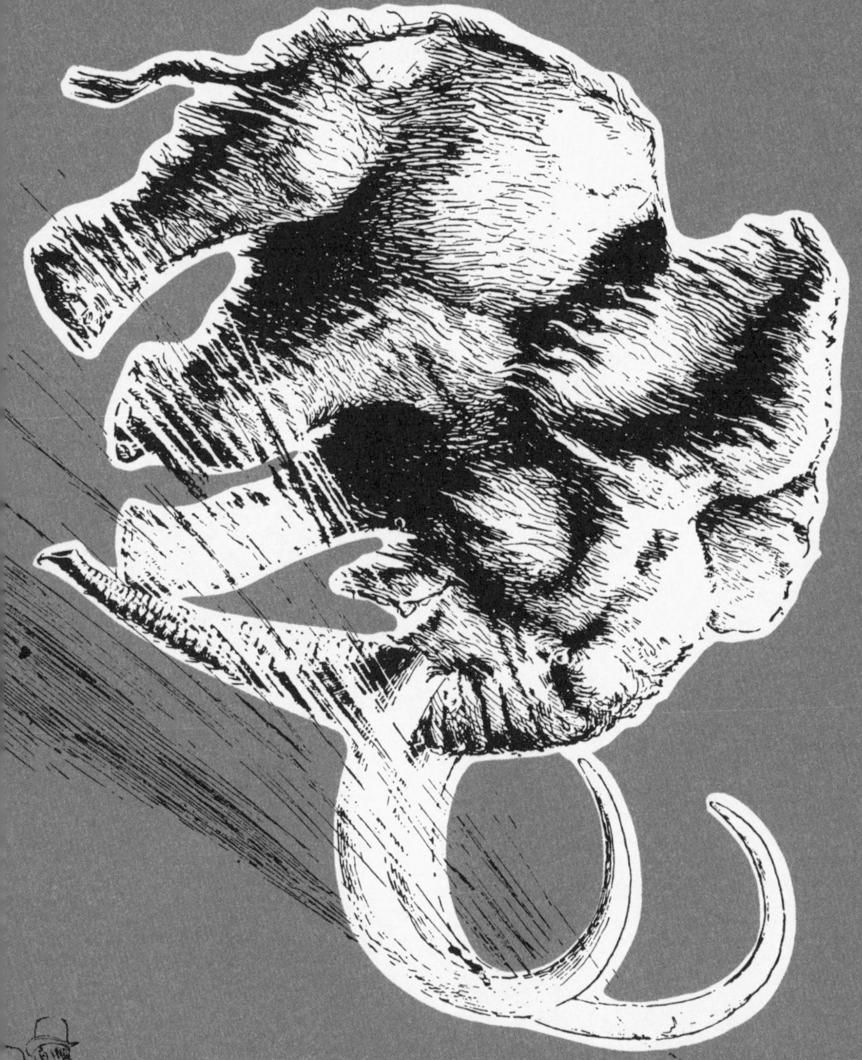

"And this is where we keep our fabulous treasure. The Gray Room. We call it the Gray Room because it doesn't make us happy, particularly."

"It's very fabulous, all the same," Mathilda agreed.

"But here is something even more fabulous!" the djinn announced. "Lunch!"

Mathilda, the djinn, and the pirate sat down to lunch. There was Fried Lobster, Fried Rice, Fried Snow Peas, and Sweet and Sour Ice Cream. The djinn gave Mathilda a glass of wine mixed with a little water, in djinn fashion.

Carte des Vins

VINS ROUGES

	La Bouteille
Ordinaire......	» 60

BOURGOGNE

Mâcon ordinaire.	1	»
» vieux....	1	50
Moulin-à-Vent..	2	50
Beaune ordinaire	2	50
Fleury.........	3	»
Pomard........	3	50
Chambertin.....	5	»

BORDEAUX

Ordinaire......	1	25
Médoc	2	50
Pomerol.......	2	50
Pontet-Canet....	3	»
Saint-Julien.....	3	50
Saint-Émilion...	4	»
Saint-Estèphe...	4	»
Château-Léoville	5	»

VINS BLANCS

	La Bouteille
Ordinaire	» 60

Chablis.........	1	»
» vieux ...	1	50
Graves ordinaire	1	50
Sainte - Foy.....	2	»
Pouilly........	2	50
Barsac	3	50
Sauterne	4	»
Haut-Sauterne ..	5	»

CHAMPAGNE

Trémant........	3 »
Grand Mousseux	4
Mercier & Cie ...	5
Ay Mousseux ...	6
Montebello	7
Rœderer & Cie...	7
Moët & Chandon	8
Pommery.......	8

QUESNEL   A. CIRALDON

PERPENDICULARITY

After lunch came the Entertainment. There were jug-dancers and clowns and elegant fencers and every kind of flawless flourishy footlooseness.

"If there is anything better than lunch, it is Entertainment," the djinn said.

"Fopderol!" the pirate cried. "If I had my cutlass back, I'd show those skinny ninnies something about cut-and-thrust!"

"Would you like to have an escapade?" the djinn asked.
"We can arrange that. Escapades come in two styles—
fancy and more fancy."

"What is an escapade?" Mathilda asked.

"An escapade is something you didn't expect," the djinn
said, "which surprises you, pleases you, and frightens you,
all at once."

"Like a good dream," Mathilda said.

"Or you could *be* something," the djinn suggested. "You could be a grown-up tennis-playing hat-wearing woman, or a one-man band—"

"The one-man band doesn't look too happy," Mathilda observed.

"He began as a piccolo player," the djinn said.

PEOPLE'S VOICE

"Now we'll have to give you a souvenir," said the djinn. "Would you like a barrel of pickles surmounted by a sour and severe citizen? Or a statue of the Chief of Police, heroic style, solid marble?"

"I'm awfully fond of fire engines," Mathilda said.

"Or a popcorn-making machine," the djinn went on, "capacity 50,000 kernels, or an anatomical diagram?"

"The anatomical diagram is anatomicomical," Mathilda said. "And the popcorn-making machine is useful, I don't doubt. But you wouldn't have a . . ."

"I am tired of talking about fire engines," the djinn said firmly.

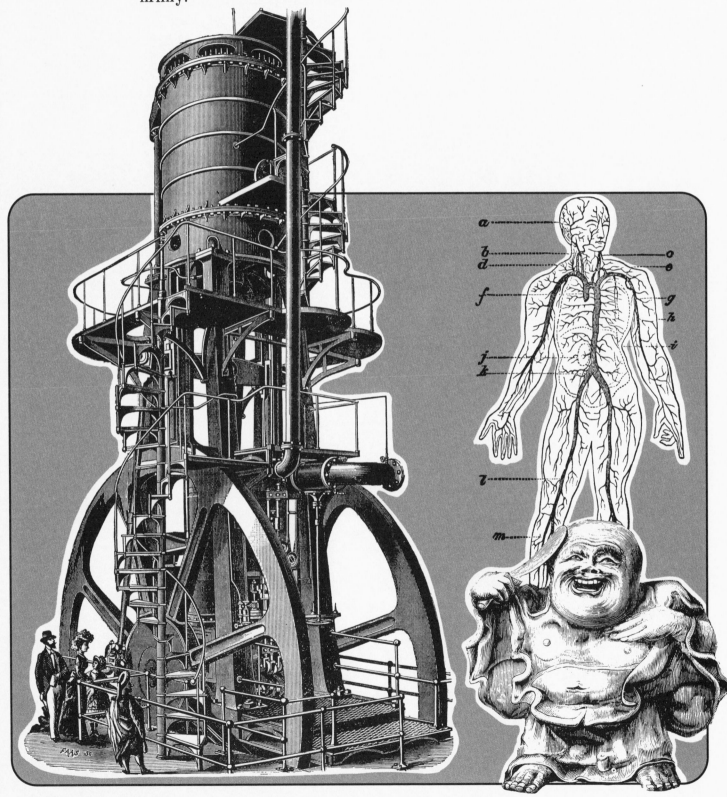

Just then a voice was heard, outside the pagoda.

"Mathilda!" the voice screamed. "Mathilda! Mathilda
Mathilda Mathilda Mathilda Mathilda Mathilda Mathilda
Mathilda Mathilda Mathilda Mathilda Mathilda Mathilda
Mathilda Mathilda Mathilda Mathilda Mathilda Mathilda
Mathilda Mathilda Mathilda Mathilda Mathilda Mathilda
Mathilda Mathilda Mathilda Mathilda Mathilda Mathilda
Mathilda Mathilda Mathilda Mathilda *Mathilda!*"

"That's my nurse," Mathilda said. "I think she wants me. Will you be here tomorrow?"

"No," the djinn said. "We're taking a trip. All the way to Pernambuco."

"The house too?"

"The house too. But we'll leave you a keepsake, Mathilda. Some little something. It will be here when you wake up tomorrow."

"Goodbye," Mathilda said. "Thank you for the . . . *escapade*."

When Mathilda woke the next morning and rushed out into the yard, the mysterious Chinese house was gone. The djinn was gone, the pirate was gone, the elephant was gone, and the two fierce-looking Chinese guards were gone.

But standing where the Chinese house had been was a magnificent new fire engine, a real Silsby. But instead of being sparkling red, it was bright green.

"The djinn must not know too much about fire engines," Mathilda thought. "But green is a beautiful color too."

And Mathilda's father and mother, that gay and laughing couple, were very glad to have a bright green fire engine to ride in when they went out for an evening, and Mathilda lent it to them whenever they wished.

CONTENTMENT
Industry and Frugality